the Enchanted Land

A Land of Faith,
Love, and Betrayal

Vicky Wells

Outskirts Press, Inc.
Denver, Colorado

The Enchanted Land
A Land of Faith, Love, and Betrayal
All Rights Reserved.
Copyright © 2008 Vicky Wells
V3.0

Cover Photo © 2008 JupiterImages Corporation. All rights reserved - used with permission.

Outskirts Press, Inc.
http://www.outskirtspress.com

Paperback ISBN: 978-1-4327-3135-9
Hardback ISBN: 978-1-4327-3175-5

Library of Congress Registration: 2008936709

Outskirts Press and the "OP" logo are trademarks belonging to Outskirts Press, Inc.

PRINTED IN THE UNITED STATES OF AMERICA

Dedication

When you gazed upon the mountains, the rivers, and the majestic land here in Georgia, there was a sparkle that beamed from your eyes. I knew you could feel the presence of our Native ancestors. Your spirit was one with theirs. You wore your black hair and dark skin like a priceless badge of honor. I wish you were here to read my book. I think you would be proud.

I dedicate this book to Ronald Morgan, my dad.

Preface

I began researching my Native American ancestry a few years ago. My father had spoken about his great, great grandmother many times throughout his life. The stories of our Cherokee heritage had been passed down for generations. Despite my research, I was unable to find any direct evidence of our Native ancestors, but I knew it was true. The physical characteristics and inherent knowledge of the land that many in my family possess had always been proof enough, but as time passed, I wanted more. I wanted evidence. So, I obtained the controversial DNA testing, which provided the written and scientific proof I needed.

I was very disappointed that I couldn't find my Indian ancestors' names on any of the Cherokee Rolls. A close friend of mine, also from Georgia, is a card-carrying member of the tribe. For a while I envied her, but later realized I didn't need a card in order to love and respect my own Indian heritage. I only wish I had listened more to the stories my family told. By the time I began this research, those who could have given me the information I needed had passed away. I encourage anyone who wants to know your heritage, please do it while the older family members are still around to help you. Their knowledge is invaluable. Researching my heritage has been such a wonderful experience.

It is that research that inspired me to write this book. I have combined some history, family stories, and fictional characters to create what I hope is both entertaining and enlightening for everyone who reads it.

It is a thought-provoking look at a life scenario that could have been true for many Cherokee women during the 19th century. It is narrated by the main character, Luiza. It is her life story as only she could tell it.

Introduction

My name is Luiza "Bluebird" Jansen. It is now the year 1875. I am 86 years old. I have lived my entire life in the state of Georgia. I have known much love and much heartache in my many years. As I lie here now, aged and fragile, I am reflecting on the life I've lived, and realize I have no regrets. My life has been a beautiful and heart-wrenching saga, filled with every emotion. I have a story to tell. If you could indulge an old Indian woman for a few moments, I'd like to share it with you now...

The Journey Begins

*God places certain people in our lives and we are
connected, not by our hearts or minds, or the color
of our skin, but by our souls.*

The coming together of the Cherokees and the
European settlers brought with it innumerable re-
wards. We learned from each other's culture, things that
enhanced the subsistence of our two worlds. In so many
cases as in mine, love formed between us as we embraced
each other's differences.

As a child I watched the relationship between my father and the white settlers we were so fond of grow in a
mutual appreciation for one another. In my innocence I believed all white people were kind. I found out quickly this

was not the case. I never dreamed the coming together of these two worlds would create one of the saddest and most heartbreaking moments in history.

The colors of the sky, the enormity of the trees, the mountains that seemed to reach the heavens were more beautiful and breathtaking than words could describe. All this could be seen in the region where my family lived, the place my people called "The Enchanted Land."

This land, the land of our ancestors, had been shared, sold, and traded for many years with the white settlers. Many Cherokees wanted to trade with the white man and learn his ways. Cherokees wanted the white man to learn their ways, too. That was not the objective for some of the white settlers. They wanted the land, no matter what was lost by the Indians in the process.

Until the white man came, Indians did not own nor did we believe we could own the land. It was a gift from the Creator. We could hear His voice in the whistling wind, the rustling leaves of the trees, in the flowing rivers and streams. We closed our eyes, and with deep, methodic breaths we could smell His perfume, the scent of all the splendor that surrounded us. We only took from this gift what we needed, and anything we could give back to the earth, we did so with thanksgiving. I only wish more whites could have understood the power in that connection.

We had formed bonds with many white families; one in particular was the Jansen family. They were of Dutch descent and lived just a short distance from our Cherokee village. They visited us often, and were welcomed into our village with open arms. Many of the Natives could speak English, including my family. We all had been given both Indian and English names.

Our family and the Jansens very much respected each other except for one of their sons, Henry. He didn't care for our family or, it seemed, any Indian family.

Henry had a tendency to go heavy on the booze and then make ugly comments toward every Indian who passed his way. One day he spit at a man named Rolling Thunder. Henry taunted him about his long hair and told him he knew prettier women than him. Rolling Thunder calmly walked over to Henry and began hitting him with his fist until he lay bloody on the ground. Henry tried to appear tough, but he was really a coward. Some of the onlookers carried him home. He was left with cuts, scrapes, and bruises. Mrs. Jansen had to tend to his wounds for three days. I believe it took him that long to sober up. He didn't even remember what happened.

One evening as I was walking by the river, just before dusk, someone jumped from behind a bush and grabbed me. I began kicking him and screaming. He slung me around and I was facing him. It was Henry. I could smell the liquor on his breath. I fought him with every ounce of strength I had, but he just kept forcing me down harder. I was able to pick up a rock and strike him with enough force that I busted his nose and broke his tooth. That made him more determined to have what he wanted. I knew I couldn't stop fighting him even if it killed me. Suddenly, someone else was there. He pulled Henry off of me and began beating him. It was James, Henry's brother. Henry began yelling, "Why are you defending that damn Indian? I wanted to show her who's boss. Just let me have my way with her, and then you can have her, too."

With every nasty word Henry spoke, James would hit him again, and each blow was harder than the last. Henry crawled away on his hands and knees as fast as he could, glancing back at James with a horrified look on his face. Once Henry disappeared into the forest, James came over and asked if I was alright. He then picked me up and carried me home. He and I didn't speak a word to each other.

He just placed me at the door of our house. I silently wept throughout the night, praying that God would comfort me. I didn't tell my family or the Jansens what Henry had done.

The next morning Mr. Jansen came to us and said that Henry had not returned home that evening. They feared something had happened to him. Mr. Jansen said he was drunk and belligerent when he stumbled away from the house. They asked my parents if we could help search for him. Of course, they said yes. As we were walking out, I saw James. I hoped he wouldn't tell what Henry had tried to do to me. He looked up at me, and I knew by the look on his face it was our secret. I saw the sadness in his eyes. I could see the pain he felt, knowing his brother could do such terrible things, and he was saying with those eyes how sorry he was that Henry had hurt me. I think it was that deplorable incident that bonded James and me for life.

Indians and whites gathered together to search for Henry. After many hours of searching the woods and river-bank, I saw it. It was his body floating down the river. I yelled for my father to come. He immediately jumped in and pulled him out of the water. Henry had been severely beaten and stabbed. He was barely recognizable. They carried his swollen and marred body home and began preparing him for burial.

We never found out who murdered him, but everyone, including the Jansens, believed it was an Indian. I remember looking at James and praying that he hadn't killed his own brother, but I never asked and we never spoke of it. The Jansens assumed he probably offended someone outside the village who didn't know him, and that person took his life. All of us knew that the hate and indifference Henry carried in his heart was ultimately responsible for his death.

The Jansens grieved their loss and buried their son. They felt only remorse for the way he treated the Natives and became even more determined to promote peace between us.

For months I had nightmares about that night and what could have occurred had James not stopped Henry. With many prayers, the nightmares became less and less, but I couldn't stop thinking about James. Every time we saw each other, there was a look of affection between us. The unspoken connection we had was obvious to everyone. My sisters sensed it and so did my brother Thomas, whom we also called Young Feather. My brother didn't agree with the relationships we had with the European settlers, so he definitely didn't like what he saw between James and me.

But Thomas was different from Henry. Thomas didn't have an evil or hateful bone in his body. He was just cautious and didn't want to see me used by a white man. If he had only known what this white man had done for me, he would have never questioned it. Thomas finally came around and accepted the Jansens as our friends. He actually became very fond of James.

James was handsome and very tall. He had the most amazing blue eyes. I had never seen eyes that color before. After a while I began imagining how it would feel to be held in his arms. I found myself in this imaginary embrace on many occasions. I had a constant longing for that man.

We were able to teach our white friends about our agriculture, the three sisters: corn, beans, and squash. They joined our tribe during the Green Corn Festival. This festival was held when the first green shoots appeared. The shamans (medicine men) chanted, and the warriors would dance around the cooking fire with cornstalks in their hands. They then boiled the ears and gave them as a sacred offering to the Great Spirit, thanking Him for the harvest. It was a time of renewal and new beginnings. The festival would last for three to four days. I think the Jansens really enjoyed participating in the festivities. They told us it was mesmerizing watching the Natives dance. The dances were very powerful. They recognized the spirituality within them. Every dancer felt closer to the Creator during the ritual. It was a celebration of gratitude for the provisions given us by the Great Creator. Mrs. Jansen commented, "We should all be as spiritually energetic and eager to express our thanks to God for the nourishment he provides."

My mother's name was Sarah. She offered to teach Mrs. Jansen how to cook the scrumptious vegetables we grew. Mrs. Jansen hesitantly said she would like to learn. I think she was a little afraid of my mother, who was a strong and independent woman. She always spoke her mind to my father if she disagreed with him. That shocked Mrs. Jansen. In the Cherokee culture, the women were respected and held in high regard. It was somewhat different in the white world. Men were the head of the woman, and that's how Mrs. Jansen lived her life, but I think she learned more than just cooking from my mother. We heard her, on occasion, telling Mr. Jansen a thing or two.

The Marriage

*Marriage is a bond of love, passion, and spirit. Let
no man or circumstance put asunder.*

Christianity had been introduced to the Indians
several years prior. My entire family was very
receptive to this faith. The white man gave us a great gift
when he brought Christianity to our culture. We didn't have
to pay for it with our land or anything else; it was free. We
would listen so intently to the stories from the Bible, and
we felt a strong relation to them. It was as though they were
speaking about our early ancestors. We also had a great
fondness for the story of Jesus. I believed he was the son of
God. For myself I felt the spirit of God take residence in

my heart, giving me a sense of belonging and comfort. I knew I loved the Great Creator God and all his wonderful gifts to us, including his Son.

One evening around my sixteenth year and James' twentieth, our mothers prepared a meal for our families to share.

After prayers of blessings in English and Cherokee, we feasted on a meal of venison, corn, squash, and bread. (We shared many meals together, these two families from different worlds.) When we had finished eating, Mr. Jansen read to us from the Bible the story of Moses and how he freed his people from bondage. That story became one of my favorites as the years passed and I witnessed the bondage of my own people.

Our parents were laughing and enjoying each other's company as the younger children played together. I was watching the children chase each other, when suddenly James asked, "Luiza, would you like to take a walk with me?"

Of course my reply was a very nervous, "Yes, I would love to."

We walked along the riverbank under the clear Georgia sky. The stars were beaming on the water as it cascaded by with its soothing sounds. It was those sights and sounds that gave you the sense of the Creator's presence in your midst. It was the very essence of our Enchanted Land.

Suddenly James said, in a gentle voice, "Luiza, you are very beautiful. I love the darkness of your skin, the way your long braids lie against your face, and the mighty spirit I see in your eyes. You are the most attractive woman in the whole village. But more than your beauty, I love your kindness, your courage, your strength, and your heart. My soul aches to be a part of yours."

He leaned over and kissed me. That was my first real kiss, but it was such a passionate kiss, it left me breathless. My parents would have never approved. I wasn't concerned. I enjoyed it. I didn't want it to end, but James pulled away, took my face in his hands, and said, "I want to be with you in every way for the rest of our lives. Luiza, will you marry me?"

I was in shock. My thoughts were racing through my mind of all I wanted to say, but the words wouldn't leave my mouth. After what seemed like several minutes, James asked again, "Well, will you be my wife?"

Finally, I began to scream, "Yes, yes, I would love to be your wife!"

James lifted me above his head and began twirling me around, and suddenly we both fell to the ground with a thump. We were laughing like children until our eyes met. He kissed me again, but with even more passion than the first time. We regained our composure and headed back to the village.

From that point on, James would often refer to me as his "Pretty Little Indian Princess."

James was so nervous to ask my father and mother for my hand. Somehow he mustered up the courage that very night. To our surprise they both said yes, but my father asked me to make him a promise. "Never lose the heritage that you were given at birth. Always remember who you are and never deny it. Share it with your children and grandchildren."

I promised him I would cherish my heritage for myself, my children, and theirs. I told him emphatically, "I will never forget that I am a Cherokee woman."

In the two weeks prior to the wedding, I was in a daze. I could not focus on anything. I seemed to daydream constantly. I couldn't believe I was about to marry the man I loved. I can't recall the number of times my mother would yell, "Bluebird, you better fly back down to earth and get those chores done!" My mind would wander to thoughts of James, no matter what I was doing.

James was also distracted. He had attended a hunting trip with my brother and several other Native men from our village. When they returned, the whole lot of them mocked poor James shamelessly. Young Feather said (amid his hysterical laughter) that James had nearly shot himself in the foot.

I was afraid this humiliation would make him decide not to marry me. He assured me it would take more than a bunch of "laughin' Injuns" to keep him from becoming my husband.

James was so different from other men, white or Native. He had a sensitive soul. He was truly kind and compassionate. He also had a strong faith in God, which gave me cause to love him even more.

The wedding day finally came. James and I were a basket of nerves. We actually had two weddings. So you can only imagine how we felt that day.

We had a Christian wedding in which we were married by a reverend who was a friend of the Jansens. He read from the Bible and asked us to say our vows. We promised to love, honor, and cherish each other until death do we part. Our eyes locked and at that moment I knew this man was God's gift to me. The love we saw in each other's eyes that day was the same love that would carry us throughout our life together. When the reverend said, "I now pronounce you husband and wife," we kissed and cried all at the same time. I turned around to see both our mothers crying, too.

We immediately went over to be married in the traditional Cherokee ceremony performed by an Indian priest. James presented me with venison and promised to be the hunter and provider for me always. He then added that he would always keep me safe. I presented him with corn, with the promise that as his wife I would always provide him with nourishment and support. We were then wrapped together in one blanket as we drank from the wedding vase at the same time. We were now sealed as husband and wife.

We were from two different worlds, but on that day we became one in the presence of God, whites, and Cherokees.

We were then led into a hut prepared especially for our wedding night. I was very anxious. I wasn't sure what to expect. I had read the book in the Bible, Song of Songs, written by King Solomon. The fourth chapter is about the marriage consummation. The aesthetic depiction of Solomon coming into the garden of his wife and her accepting him into her garden gave me a visual sense of what making love was, and it comforted me as I became my husband's lover. The experience we had together was more beautiful than even Solomon's exquisite description. I was amazed that God spoke of such things. It was more evidence that through His Word, He provides for every need.

And Two Make Seven

From the moment of your birth came glorious sing-
ing from the heavens and from my grateful heart.

I n 1806, we had our first child, William, strong and handsome, just like his father, with the radiant copper glow of the Cherokee and those piercing blue eyes. You can only imagine how handsome he was. We would go on to have six more children and twenty-five grandchildren in our life together.

In 1807, we had another bundle of joy, or little papoose as James liked to call them. He just loved that word. The child was another boy. We named him Jacob.

We had another child in March of 1808 named Elijah.

James said he reckoned I was just a baby maker. I reckon he was right. By 1813, we had three more children, James Jr., Thomas, and John.

We had continued to live in the village near my parents, but James wanted to buy property in Bells County. He had saved some money and found the perfect place. It was a plentiful land with 130 acres for farming and raising cattle, a place he felt he could be his own man and raise his children.

He knew I didn't want to go, but he also knew I loved him enough to follow him anywhere. He believed he could give his family a good and prosperous life there.

James left our home to prepare for us a new home in Bells. He was gone for over seven months. We only got word about him from one of the villagers who had gone down to help him. He came back to see his family, but James would not come. He wanted to have the house built and the land ready for planting before he returned for us. I was so desperate to see his face and feel his arms around me. The children cried for him almost every night. I had such a sad and weary heart. I needed my husband home.

I didn't know it when he left, but I was pregnant again. I felt I would no more birth one child till I was pregnant with the next. I really did feel my role in life was to be a baby maker, but I didn't mind. I counted all my children as wonderful and amazing blessings from God.

I was several weeks from my delivery date when I began having pain. This pain I knew all too well. My baby was going to be born soon and way too early.

Father went for the shaman on the other side of town. He was one of a very few practicing shamans at the time. He had been present for the birth of all my children. He always prepared a special tea that the children would drink for seven days before I was allowed to nurse them. This was to protect them from evil spirits and illness.

When he arrived, the time was near for delivery. My mother and Mrs. Jansen were there to help me deliver this special child. The shaman prayed and chanted in our native language as Mrs. Jansen and my mother prayed over me. My father and siblings were right outside waiting in silence for the birth of my baby. My heart longed for James so much, but my focus had to be on the task at hand. I said a quick prayer for strength as I pushed my baby girl into the world.

The delivery went quickly because the baby was so small. I asked God to please hear my voice and save my child. She was small, but amazingly appeared very healthy.

I held her close as the shaman prepared a very special tea for this child and began placing it on her tongue. He said it would help the Great Spirit finish the growth of this tiny baby, which had begun in my womb, but would now have to be completed outside in the world. He said that after the seven days I could nurse, but to continue giving her the special tea for one month. He said this was told to him by the Great Spirit.

To this day I don't know what was in that medicine, but it, along with all the prayers, saved my baby daughter. I named her Lucinda, after James' grandmother. I knew this would make him happy. Our Lucinda grew fast and was strong, healthy, and beautiful, just like her brothers.

James was not aware of the newest member of our family. When he returned, I welcomed him home by placing our little girl in his arms. It was obvious he was astonished by what he saw. He just stood there with his mouth to the floor, completely speechless. Finally, he began to cry. Then of course we all began to cry, including Lucinda. As we turned to go into the house, James smiled at me and said, "I love you, Mrs. Jansen. My baby makin' Indian princess."

Immediately, I responded, "Guess what, Mr. Jansen, my white prince, you are a baby maker, too. I couldn't make these babies alone."

We laughed all night from pure joy and contentment. That night we gave praises to our Lord for all our many blessings. We were so happy to be together. I made him promise to never, ever leave me like that again.

Our New Home

A woman must leave her parents for new and uncertain destinations, but a husband's smile and a child's laughter can cause joy to reign in a heavy heart.

James was ecstatic about what he had accomplished, and he shared it with anyone who would listen. He was ready to take us to our new home. I didn't share his excitement. I was scared to leave the only home I had ever known. I was nervous about departing from the comfort and safety of my village and my people for a place unknown. My parents were saddened as well, but James was my husband and my life was with him.

The time came for us to travel to our new life in Bells

County. The tears were flowing like the raging river near the place we had called home for so many years. We said good-bye to James' family. My mother hugged me and told me to remember all I had learned from living with the tribe, and continue to teach it to my children. My father kissed my forehead and reminded me of the promise I had made to him before I married James.

We finished our good-byes, placed the children into our fully loaded wagon, and began the journey to the home we would live in for the rest of our lives.

On the journey we talked, laughed, and sang hymns. This helped to pass the many hours spent on the rocky dirt roads. The children did exceptionally well. They endured all the bumps and even some rain along the way, and never complained. They were excited about the changes we were about to experience.

We finally arrived after our seventy-mile trip. I had the comfort of knowing that we were close enough to visit our families from time to time. James stopped the wagon in front of the most amazing house I had ever seen. The children jumped from the wagon and began running from room to room, shouting, "Papa, this is the best house in the whole world!"

I had to agree with them. I had never seen anything as grand as that house. It had columns on the front, like the large plantation houses I had seen on the way. My favorite room was the kitchen. James had built it just the way he knew I would want it. It was perfect. The wood-burning stove was large enough for all my cooking needs. It was cast iron with white doors. It had no resemblance to the rickety stoves I had been accustomed to, but it didn't take me long to learn how to use it. James even had enough wood piled on the porch for a month of cooking and heating. He had also built a cold cellar for our meat with meat hooks already built in. He had even built three barns on the property for our animals. It was obvious how hard he had worked.

We were all very pleased with what James had done. I could tell by the smile on his face he was pleased with himself, too.

We spent the next several weeks working very hard to get the fields planted and feeding the cows. James had bought the cows the day we got there. We made our living raising and selling cattle. We had a small garden that fed our family. I pampered it and called it mine. I treated that garden as though it were one of my children. I wore calloused hands from clearing the weeds every day. It was quite the garden if I do say so myself. Even my children were impressed with it, especially at mealtime. They said I cooked better than Granny Sarah. Now that was a real compliment.

We were a hardworking family, including the children. We rose early every morning. After eating a hearty breakfast, we all went to work on the farm. The children helped to feed and water the cows, in the morning and at night. They were so cute throwing hay bales that were bigger than they were. But they didn't mind; they quite enjoyed being a part of it. We also had several chickens. As Lucinda got older, she loved to help with them while the boys tended the cattle. She and I would gather eggs together every day. She would help me out in my garden, too. I taught her how to plant, when to plant, and when to harvest. I learned from my tribal family that you work together for the good of the entire tribe. This was the way I demanded my family live our lives. We worked together, played together, and prayed together. I know the success we had in our lives was due to this belief.

James received word that someone was selling a sawmill a few miles down the road. He wanted that sawmill to be his. He came to discuss it with me, and I was apprehensive. I worried that it would fail. I worried how we would run the farm without him there during the day. He understood my fears and said he wouldn't mention it again. I saw the disappointment all over his face, but being the man he was, he let it go because he cared so much about my feelings. I realized most men didn't even ask the opinions of their wives in such matters, much less actually listen to them. As I have said before, James wasn't like most men. I knew how much it really meant to him, so one night after dinner I asked him how we could make it happen. He knew exactly what I was talking about and smiled his beautiful smile as he kissed my cheek. We then went over some ways we could get the money to buy it. We sold twenty acres of our land to a chicken farmer. I made blankets and weaved baskets every day, which I took into town to sell. They sold very quickly. The wealthy white women loved to buy goods that had been handmade by an Indian.

We were able to come up with all we needed within a month. His dream of owning that sawmill came true.

Owning the business meant we had to undergo some changes at home. James would be working long hours. He had to hire men to work our fields and tend our cows. I was in charge of all the sales that were made. James didn't want anyone outside the family dealing with our money. He always called it ours, and he always made sure men treated me just as they would him, but with much more respect. Most of the men didn't like making business deals with a woman, nor did they want to hand over their money to one, much less an Indian woman. They finally grew accustomed to doing business with me, becoming regular buyers and even referring other buyers to us. I was accepted; at least I felt accepted, whether I actually was or not.

James was able to round up several workers for the mill. He treated all his employees fairly. He never had a man quit. Everyone around knew James' reputation and wanted to work for him.

Some of the wealthy farmers owned black slaves. James and I didn't and would have never owned a slave. We thought it to be immoral. How could you buy a person? Some Cherokees had slaves. I was ashamed of the ones who did, and I told them so. God did not create human beings to be bought and sold like cattle. We had no need for servants. If there was something we couldn't take care of ourselves, then we would hire someone to do it for us.

The business became a quick success. James wasn't

very educated, but he could read some, sign his name, and count out a week's pay to every worker without one mistake. To me he was the smartest man I ever met, next to my father.

Our successful businesses gave us the ability to indulge in certain pleasures we had not known before. In the past, the children wore moccasins I had made for them, but now we could buy them a pair of store-bought shoes every year at the General Store in town. James would surprise me with gifts that only wealthy white women had been privy to, such as large beaded hats and lace dresses. I truly felt like a princess.

The Birth of Lulabell

New life springs forth from all creations.

I n the spring we had several cows expecting around the same time. One in particular had begun her labor that afternoon. The cows usually delivered their calves just fine on their own. Occasionally, we had to assist those in distress. That evening a terrible storm came, with wind, lightning, and hard rain. We could hear the mother screeching over the sound of the severe weather outside, and we knew she was in trouble. James was still at the mill. I had to take care of this myself.

I gathered up the children to help me. We made our way through the storm to the barn in the east pasture where she had gone to deliver. We could hear her bellowing the entire distance from the house to the barn. She was in awful misery. I told Elijah, Jacob, John, James Jr., and Lucinda to hold her down and rub her belly. I had William and Thomas stay beside me to fetch equipment or ropes, if needed. I placed my hand inside her and realized the calf was turned sideways. If I didn't act fast, they would both die. I placed both hands inside her almost to my elbows and turned the baby calf around. I looked over at the children and saw they were all white as cotton. I found this hard to believe after I had taught all of them how to skin and dress a deer, kill and pluck chickens, and clean fresh fish. I suppose they handled that better because it was necessary for "their" survival and this wasn't.

Once I had the calf completely turned, I began to pull the legs as hard as I could. I was stronger than I realized. I had pulled with so much force, the calf came flying out and knocked me backwards. Of course, the children laughed at me until I gave them one of my famous looks, the one that says, "I'm fixin' to tan your hide."

I inspected the mama and calf. They both seemed to be fine. Before I glanced back at the children, I thought of how I must have looked when I flew across the barn holding the legs of that baby calf. I started laughing at myself. I looked over at the children and said, "I guess I did look hilarious, huh?" Then we all had a good laugh together.

They were amazed by what they had witnessed. James couldn't believe we had done it without him. All the children talked about that day for years afterward. They called it the miracle cow. We couldn't keep Lucinda away from the calf. She actually wanted to sleep with it. She treated that animal like it was a baby. One day she introduced the cow as Lulabell. After she had gone and named it, James and I didn't have the heart to take it from her. We surprised her by allowing her to keep and care for it, but it was completely her responsibility, and everyone knew that cow was to never be sold or eaten. Lucinda cared for her very well. Ms. Lulabell was part of our family until she died of old age.

More Land Cessions

Struggles with identity, the silent screams
Who am I really? Where do I belong?

I t seemed almost every day, another piece of Cherokee land was ceded to white settlers. Many tribes in the south had already ceded their land and gone to places west to start over. Most Cherokees continued to fight for their land.

A white man named Andrew Jackson was a warrior who actually fought alongside Cherokees at Horseshoe Bend against the Creeks in 1814. He and the Cherokee were allies, and he was considered a hero after this battle. We didn't have a clue that he would eventually become our worst enemy. We would later see the cold heart of this man at its worst.

My parents were determined to hang on to their land, but it was a never-ending battle, as it was for all the Cherokee tribe. The white settlers and traders were constantly trying to convince them to give up their land for some price or another, as though they could actually put a price on such a precious gift.

Because I was married to a white man, and he was considered the property owner, we were never at risk of losing our land. I felt so guilty for having a sense of security when my people were struggling to keep what was rightfully theirs. I saw the pain it caused them. I didn't know the worst was yet to come.

By the year 1820, I had adapted quite well to the white way of life. Except for the color of my skin and the heart in my chest, I lived the life of a white woman. I had not given up all the ways of an Indian woman, but I dressed white and spoke white and lived as a white woman married to a white man. I had his name. I spoke his language, except to our children. I didn't want them ever to lose our native language. They could speak fluently in English and Cherokee. I taught them all the Native ways just as I had promised my father I would, yet we didn't live them. We lived the white way.

People were less accepting of Indians than they had been in the past. Being considered white made my life easier, but I felt a sickness in my stomach that never went away. It was for the heritage I felt slipping away from me little by little. If it weren't for the periodic visits to see my family, I believe I would have lost even more of the heritage that I was so proud of and that brought so much beauty into my world. I lived in two worlds. I was very happy in the one, but always longed for the other. I hid my pain, but some days were very difficult. The yearning in my heart for the way of life I knew was at times overwhelming, but the love I had for James was so deep, I couldn't allow this pain to fill my thoughts. If I had allowed it to, I would have been betraying James and the sweet love we shared.

I had a wonderful life there, but I was never so completely happy and so completely sad at the same time. I never told James my true feelings. If he had known what I really felt inside my soul, it would have placed his in anguish, too.

Teaching the Children

*Give them the tools so they may be prepared to take
on this world of obstacles with the confidence and
clarity to obtain their goals, dreams, and aspirations.*

J ames and I argued over the children getting an education. He didn't think it was necessary to learn reading
and writing. He believed since he had survived well with
very little schooling, our children would, too. I disagreed
with him, and after much discussion on the matter, I was
able to persuade him to allow me to teach the children at
night after the day's work and chores were completed.

I could read and write in English. I learned from a
wealthy white family named Johnson that Father had met

when I was a young girl. He traded deerskins, baskets, and bows and arrows with them in exchange for my education, and that of my brothers and sisters.

I taught William and the rest of the children how to read and write from the books I had been given by the Johnsons. I taught them the math I knew, which wasn't much, but enough to get them by in life. They all enjoyed learning, just as I always had. After supper the children would sit at the table, ready for their lessons. Most nights it went smoothly, but sometimes Elijah and James Jr. would argue over something silly, and I would have to break it up. Of all my children, they were the only ones who ever got in trouble with either James or me. I always said it was because they were so much alike. They hated it when I said that. (Ironically, as they got older, they were closer to each other than they were to any of the other children.) John and Thomas were slower to learn, but they just worked harder to compensate. Lucinda was a girl after her mother's own heart; she loved every aspect of the learning process. She could read almost as well as I could, even when she was just a tiny little thing. Teaching my children was one of the greatest joys of my life.

William worked all day, but was always anxious to get

home to his studies. We were so proud of him. We knew one day he would do great things. He had a passion for learning about our Native culture. I spent extra time with him, teaching him about our beliefs and all the old ways of tribal life. I had no way of knowing, at that time, just how much that knowledge would benefit him in his life. Teaching him kept me grounded. It helped me to remember I was not just Luiza Jansen—I was also Bluebird, a full-blood Cherokee.

James' parents had moved down to be closer to us. Having them close by was great for all of us. Mrs. Jansen would occasionally take time from her busy day to help me teach the children. She enjoyed being there for them, and they loved having her around.

We were a happy family. All our children were healthy, including our little Lucinda. We gave thanks daily for the life we had been given. Each night we read from the Bible, then said prayers with the children and tucked them into bed. James and I would lie in bed holding each other and talking for hours about how fortunate we were. Before we fell off to sleep, he would kiss me gently and whisper in my ear how much he loved me. Having that man as my husband and father to my children truly enriched my life.

And the Journey Continues

Inside this journey are many twists and turns.
One moment is pain, the next is joy, but
knowledge can clear away the uncertainties,
if only for a moment.

B y 1824, the fight for Cherokee land had intensi-
fied. Many treaties had been signed and broken
by the white man. I never understood these things. I didn't
know what all the fuss was about. There was enough land
here for the Cherokee and whites to all have a piece. I
couldn't comprehend why they wanted the Cherokees'
land. My father continued to believe that the issues could

be resolved peacefully, and all could get the outcome they desired. He thought since he was a Christian Cherokee, this would help in trying to convince the white man to work together with the Cherokee and keep their treaties as honorable men should. His pleas continued to be unheard. He could never seem to give up his hope that somehow peace would come between the two worlds.

All this surrounded me, but I was shielded from it by the color of my husband's skin. I wasn't directly affected by it, although I did endure the occasional prejudice from the locals around where we lived. For the most part I ignored them, but I always held my head high. I hoped for the peace my father wanted, but I knew in my heart that it wasn't going to happen for my people. I had dreams and visions of horrible things that I couldn't bring myself to share with him. My senses told me terrible things were going to occur. I pushed those thoughts from my mind.

The greed that engulfed some of the white settlers was of such a magnitude that nothing could stop them from having what they wanted. They wanted all the land, and I believed they would do whatever they needed to get it. James, being white, tried to defend his people, but quickly realized that some of his people were not of great morals. He knew they were wrong, and he carried a sense of guilt because he himself was a white settler. We both agreed that we could not judge all whites the same, no more than anyone could judge all Natives the same. Some were of Godly morals with kind hearts, and some were not. For some people, no matter the color of their skin, greed controlled their inner beings.

William had become involved in the process of trying to save what land was left for the Cherokee. He would speak with Cherokees everywhere he went, telling them not to relinquish their land no matter what was offered for it. Some listened, while others did not. He was not deterred. He was brave and steadfast in his beliefs. He encouraged his brothers and sister to keep the faith and always believe in the heritage from which they were born. Even though they were half white and half Cherokee, he wanted to make sure they honored their Native ancestors, and so did I. William was so much like his grandfather and was following in his footsteps. He was not only grateful to be the grandson of John Youngwolf, he was extremely proud to be Cherokee.

A wonderful thing happened within the Cherokee tribe. A man named Sequoyah had finished establishing a written language for the Cherokee. I, having already been educated in English, was thrilled by this accomplishment. I studied the syllabary so I could learn to write in my own language. I went on to teach it to my children. Of course, William learned it as well, but he was fortunate enough to learn it directly from Sequoyah himself. The Cherokee people were so intelligent, twenty-five percent of the tribe could already read and write. They learned the syllabary within six months.

It seemed all the laboring back and forth with the United States government and the Georgia government had finally paid off. A Sovereign Nation for the Cherokee was formed. It was believed that their land would always be their land, and the tribe thought that would be their final move. The Cherokee Nation was made up of eight districts: Hickory Log, Chatooga, Amoah, Etowah, Aquohee, Chickamauga, Tahquohee, and Coosewatee. The capital was called New Echota; it was originally called Newtown, but was later named Echota after a town called Chota in Tennessee, where many famous Cherokees were born.

The government was established using the white man's laws and courts. Cherokee government was similar to the white man's. We were completely civilized, according to the white man's standards of civilization. We had our own National Council made up of elected officials, with the Principal Chief, Assistant Principal Chief, and twelve lower members. The printing press was started, and we had our own newspaper. Shortly after it was established, private homes and stores were built, as well as the Council House and Supreme Court buildings. In the minds of all Cherokees, there would be no more reason for further land cessions.

It was very quiet in the Cherokee Nation, except when council meetings were held—then every Cherokee and their families from near and far came by foot, horseback, or wagon to attend. There would be events for everyone to participate in. William attended every council meeting. We were amazed at his maturity and resolve when it came to decisions regarding our people. He wanted to be involved and have his voice heard. James, myself, and our other children would spend time enjoying all the festivities. After the meetings were over, William and the other men would get together for a game of stick ball. My father and mother, along with all my siblings, would be there. It was one big reunion for every member of the tribe.

James was so impressed by all that the Cherokee had

accomplished. He told me he was honored to be a part of such an intelligent and loving group of people. He consistently thanked me for all he had learned from me and the values that had been instilled in our children. The love of nature and the desire for peace, along with the faith in God shared by both of us, had helped to create seven outstanding children to share in our lives of love and diversity. We both knew we had blessings beyond measure, that white man and me.

The Discovery of Gold

Greed and prejudice are a vicious combination of poison. The poison knows no boundaries; it can make its dwelling in the best of men and the worst of men. It taints all who are in its path.

By 1828, the Cherokee had a Nation, a capital, a printing press, a newspaper called the *Cherokee Phoenix*, and what seemed to be a secure life. As the past had already shown, this too would not last. That year gold was discovered in Georgia. It was on Cherokee land, inside the Cherokee Nation. This was the worst thing that could have happened to my people. The discovery set off a new level of determination for the white man to get the Indians out. They began trying more diligently to get the land. We had not yet witnessed it to this degree.

As usual these things did not affect my family directly. We stayed to ourselves as much as possible. All of us but William—he wanted to make a difference. He became even more involved in the council meetings with the Principal Chief and other officials. They were as determined not to lose the land as the whites were to get it.

Andrew Jackson had become president of the United States. In 1830, he signed into law the "Indian Removal Act." William and James had to explain to me what that meant: all Native Americans would have to cede their lands and go west of the Mississippi. It gave the government the ability to negotiate removal treaties with the Five Civilized Tribes (Cherokee, Chickasaw, Choctaw, Creek, and Seminole). Laws were passed that stated whites had to get permits to work or live in Cherokee Territory. That was an effort to also force all the missionaries to leave the Cherokee Nation. The Cherokees filed lawsuits at the US Supreme Court to stop what Georgia and the United States were trying to do. But in 1831, it was ruled that the Cherokee could not file lawsuits in the United States, nor could Cherokees testify against white men in court.

I was confused by their words. I thought they would

make me leave my husband. I suppose William saw my confused look, and he quickly responded, saying, "Mother, this will not affect you because Papa is white and he owns the property. It is the Cherokee land they're after, not the land owned by white men. They won't force the Indian wives of white men to go."

I should have been relieved by his statement, but I wasn't.

My Native family and friends tried to comprehend all that was happening. They all wanted to believe that this was a bad dream (it was mine, the one I'd been having for years). They all believed this, too, would pass and that Georgia wouldn't be allowed to so blatantly force them from their home.

Ironically, the whites still tried to treat us as uncivilized people with no rights, even though the Cherokee were civilized, with our own established government, leaders, and laws. It was humiliating and disheartening to see how our people were being treated after all those achievements.

Some Cherokees felt ceding all the remaining land and going out west was in the best interest of the tribe. Most of the Cherokees disagreed, including the Principal Chief at the time. A proponent of the land cessation was the publisher of the *Cherokee Phoenix* newspaper. Because of his views, he was pressured by the Principal Chief to resign his post.

The Cherokee continued to fight through appeals to the government against the Removal Act. Many people were arrested for their efforts. The Cherokee Nation was forced to disseminate. The council meetings were still held but were moved to Tennessee. William continued to be a vital part of the tribal functions and followed them to the new council grounds at Red Clay, but even there they were arrested by the Georgia Guard. William was among those arrested. James tried to get him out of their jail, but they would not allow it. I was so upset and angry at the government of Georgia. I was infuriated that they would actually arrest them. I believe that was the first time I became that angry. My blood was boiling, and I literally wanted to hurt someone. James spent hours trying to settle me down. William was released a week later.

My father and mother continued to live on their land and in their home. Some of those within the village had already left for the west. My family was holding out to see if the situation would change.

In 1835, a treaty was negotiated and signed by three

prominent members of the tribe. The treaty stated that the Cherokee were to cede all the remaining land for a relatively small amount of money and a guaranteed area of land west of the Mississippi in what was already considered Indian Territory. These men did not go before the council. They made this decision and signed the treaty without conferring with the Principal Chief or anyone else within the tribe. That fact should have rendered the treaty illegal, and it should have been abolished. Again, the Principal Chief tried to fight it, this time by going to Washington. He wanted to speak directly to the president, but they refused to allow him inside. There were no further legal actions that could be taken against the government, in spite of the illegal action taken against the Indians. William said we now had to accept defeat and ready ourselves for what was to come.

The deadline for the voluntary removal was May 23, 1838. The Cherokees who remained on this date would be forcibly removed.

My mind knew what was happening, but my heart didn't want to believe it. In spite of all that had occurred over the years, none of us really thought the Natives could be forced out of Georgia.

My father was especially distraught over the reality he had to face after years of struggling to keep the land he so cherished.

Many of the Natives who had not previously gone out west decided to concede defeat and move out on their own. My Native family would not go until they were forced. Father told all of us he would stay right up until the very end. He always said a true warrior may be defeated, but he would not saunter from his home with his head hung down. He said he wouldn't fight or endanger the family but that he would stay as long as possible, and then when the time came, he would leave this place he loved with his head held high as a man of honor, not of humiliation.

Our Woeful Good-bye

How can we accept defeat in this battle?
Did we really have a chance to win?
Can we say good-bye when we really don't
want to go? Is betrayal the unspoken word
that echoes silently in our heads?

illiam had been so focused on the work he was doing for the tribe that he never made time for anything else. He was still alone. He had not even made time to become acquainted with any lady friends. By that point, we had hoped he would at the least have a prospect for marriage, but he didn't. After there were no more council meetings or work to be done, his mind continued to stay on the troubles of the Cherokee. He was distressed and anxious all the time. For three years he seemed to wander aimlessly. He didn't quite know what to do with himself. So he worked at the mill with James and helped around the farm. He carried a look of sadness on his face that never faded. Occasionally, while watching his nieces and nephews play, he would break into laughter, but it was temporary. James and I prayed for him every night. We asked God to grant him peace so he could enjoy the blessings we did have, and the most important of these blessings was each other.

James and I lived our lives one day at a time. We spent time with our children and grandchildren. We visited my Native family often. We knew the time was coming that we wouldn't be able to see them for a long while.

On May 1, 1838, we began our final trip to my parents' home. It took four wagons to carry our large family on the seventy-mile trek. Our grandchildren were as well behaved as our children had always been. It was an uneventful trip, except all the grandchildren wanted to ride in the wagon with Papa James and Grandma Lu. Of course there wasn't enough room, so we had crying children for a few miles.

When we arrived, my parents met us at the door. They were always overjoyed when we came to visit. Father gave the children candy, something they very rarely got at our house. He looked at the children through glassy, tear-filled eyes. He tried to wipe them away and stand up straight and stoic so they wouldn't see. They were consumed by the treasures they had been given, so they didn't notice his sorrow, but I did. I took his hand in mine. We didn't speak, but our eyes met and we saw each other's heartache. No words were necessary.

We spent the days that followed praying together. Sometimes we cried together. That visit was different from the other visits. There wasn't as much laughter as there had always been before, and although we tried to make it enjoyable, pain was a defining presence in all of us.

It was time for us to leave, to return to our safe little world. I tried to convince my family to come to our home and escape this nightmare. My father would not hear of it. He said they would find him and make him go. He looked at my mother and all my Native family and said to me, "James and his white skin can protect you, but it cannot protect us from this inevitable fate."

William refused to return with us. He believed it was also his fate to go with the tribe to the new land. He wanted to go with my father. I begged him to come back with us, but he stood firm in his conviction to stand by the tribe and my father. I had to respect him as the strong man of courage he was and let him go.

It was so difficult for me to kiss my precious son good-bye, but I knew how he felt inside. He had to follow his heart. He kissed me on the cheek and told me he loved me. He went to shake his father's hand, but James grabbed him around the neck and hugged that big boy harder than he ever had before. He told William how proud he was of the man he had become.

After all our good-byes, I had to climb into that wagon and leave my family there to endure alone the heartache of the events about to unfold. My father said he felt like he was abandoning his beloved home. I felt like I was abandoning them.

On the trip back, I told James we should go out west with them. "They are my family and I am theirs. I am Cherokee and should suffer the same consequences as they are being forced to suffer." James would not go back. He didn't want to give up the life he had made for us here. He told me how much he loved me, but going out west with the tribe was not an option.

The Inevitable Comes

*My God, in the face of these uncertainties I will
trust you. Reveal to me the things I do not know,
give me courage to endure the truth.*

I knew my father would stay until the deadline date. So when May 23rd came, I lay crying in my bed, not knowing what my family would be enduring at that moment. My pain was almost unbearable. James tried to comfort me, but there was nothing he could have done to ease the burden I held in my heart. I didn't want to get up, and I didn't want to talk to anyone. It was days before I snapped out of my depression and began functioning again.

When James knew I was emotionally strong enough, he

told me that he had heard stories that soldiers had taken families from their homes at gunpoint and forced them to stockades, where they would stay until it was time for them to leave for the west. He said they were herded like cattle instead of human beings. On hearing those words, I began to beg God to please protect my family. Praying was the only thing I could do for them now.

There was a woman I would see on the road from time to time as she passed our farm. She and her family had a farm a short distance from ours. I had always waved to her as she walked by, but had never actually spoken to her. She was a very cordial lady with a kind smile. On this particular day, she stopped by to speak with me. She introduced herself as Mattie and said her husband was a soldier for the army and had been assigned to the removal. I felt my temperature starting to boil, and she could see how uncomfortable I was when she revealed that information. She immediately explained why she was there. Mattie looked at me with such tenderness and said, "I know your family is probably in one of the stockades now. I just want you to know that my husband is a kind, compassionate man. I know if he sees your family, he will treat them well. I hope that offers you a little peace of mind."

I was touched by her concern, and I thanked her. I asked her if she had heard any more news about what had happened during and since the removal. She was hesitant to tell me at first. I had to assure her I was alright and that she could share all she knew.

She said that several Cherokees had escaped into the mountains of North Carolina and were hiding out there. (They were eventually allowed to stay and live on their own reservation there.)

She told me that many of the military were not as caring as her husband. Many of the Indians weren't allowed to take their belongings. They were forced out at gunpoint so quickly they couldn't even retrieve coats or shoes. One family's young son had fallen in the river and drowned on the day the soldiers came. The family had just begun preparing his body for burial when the soldiers stormed the house and demanded they move out and leave the boy. They said there was no time for a funeral. The father of the boy rushed one of the soldiers, and they shot him. The grieving woman, along with her other children, had to leave the bodies of her precious son and husband lying there.

As Mattie was telling me these things, I was battling my body; it wanted to faint, but I couldn't allow it. I needed to know the truth about what was happening to my people.

She went on to tell me of the illnesses the Indians were suffering within the stockades. Many were dying and not receiving proper medical care. She then reassured me again that her husband would do all he could to protect them, even from other soldiers who might try to harm them. She said, "I know you have never had to hide being an Indian before, but the way things are now, you had better be careful. Since your husband is Dutch, why don't you say you are Black Dutch?"

I responded to her insistently, "I will never deny my heritage, no matter what!" I then apologized for yelling at her.

She said she understood and was just concerned for my well-being. I believed her. We would go on to become close friends.

After my conversation with Mattie I began conjuring up all kinds of horrible images of what my family was going through. Those images haunted me. My family could be enduring any manner of torment from wherever they were at the hands of others, while I endured my own torment within myself.

The Deception

Should I give up or should I go on? Is my faith truly strong enough? Have I completely lost my identity or is fear defining me now? My hands reach out to you, my voice screams, my heart cries, remove my pain, my confusion.

It had been several months without word from William or my father. We had no way of knowing if they were dead or alive.

The last thing we heard was that the Principal Chief had requested they be allowed to conduct their own removal to the west without the assistance of the military. His request had been granted. They were to begin their journey from the stockades to the new Indian Territory in October of that year. We were told it would take the wagons months to get there. That year the winter was harsh, so once again I feared for the well-being of all my Native tribe. And again all I could do was pray for their safe passage.

I continued to feel I was betraying them by staying in Georgia. James and I had become distant from each other. I knew he was carrying some guilt as well, because he knew he would not leave this land unless he, too, was forced. The burden of our guilt was taking a toll on our relationship.

Eventually, I realized I had to be strong for James and my family here. My father told me years ago being married to a white man would never be easy. I had not fully understood his words until that time. I knew my family was depending on me. I had to remain strong. They needed me and I definitely needed them. James and I assured each other that nothing could or would ever come between us. Our love was built on a rock, and no amount of adversity could separate us.

The guilt I carried was still there. Periodically it flashed through my mind and sent chills through my body. I didn't think I could do anything worse than I had already done. I was wrong.

One day, while the grandchildren and I were in town

getting supplies for the farm, some men began yelling at me. They screamed, "Why are you here! You don't belong here! You should be out west with the rest of the dirty Indians!"

As they began coming toward us, I pushed the children into the wagon. I looked back and they were getting closer. I began to yell back at them, "My name is Luiza Jansen. I am Black Dutch. I am not an Indian!" I jumped into the wagon and pounded the reins hard against the horses' backs. We had to move quickly. After we were well out of town, I stopped the wagon. I looked up to the sky and began to scream for God to forgive me. I screamed for my father and mother to forgive me. It was the ultimate deception. I had broken my promise. How could I live with myself? The children were crying. They didn't understand what was happening to me. From that point on, I believe the horses just knew the way home because I don't remember the remainder of the ride.

When the wagon stopped in front of the house, James came running out. He could hear my wails of agony and despair. He told the children to stay outside as he carried my limp body inside the house. He placed me on the bed and asked me what had happened. I told him all that had occurred and that I had betrayed my parents and all Cherokees. At that moment he stopped me and said that I had done the only thing I could have, and no matter what was done or said to either of us, we always had to protect the children. He then said he believed my people would forgive me for keeping my grandchildren free from harm. I knew he was right, but I also knew the pain of that day and what I had done would never leave me. It would forever be etched in my mind. But once again, amidst all my anguish, I dusted myself off and continued on with life.

That would not be my last time to deny who I was. Indians married to whites had to list themselves as whites whenever a census was taken. I think we were all afraid not to, for fear they would strip us from our husbands and children. James was right—that would have been harder than denying myself and my heritage. I constantly felt torn between the two worlds. I became so confused I began to wonder who I really was. I held within me a strong allegiance to both worlds.

News of the Arrival

The loss of a home so dear, the loss of a loved one,
The anguish seething from every being affected by it
The strength of the human soul has been tested and
it continues on in desperate determination.

One day in late August as I was going into the Mercantile, Mr. Macky from the post office yelled to me, "Mrs. Jansen, Mrs. Jansen, come quick." He said he had something for me. As I walked in, he handed me a letter from William.

June 1, 1839

Dear Mother,

We finally arrived in Indian Territory. It is nothing like Georgia. I don't think any place on earth could ever be as beautiful as our Native home, but we are trying to make this our new home. Please pray for us in our endeavors here. Things are not great, but I am not going into detail about it. Just know we need prayers.

Mother, I have some very sad news. It is quite hard for me to tell you this. Grandpa did not complete the journey. He got pneumonia on the trail. He succumbed to the illness and passed away. I am so sorry to relay this heartbreaking information to you this way. The rest of us are doing alright. We have had to adjust to a lot of things quickly, including the death of Grandpa. I pray you can adjust quickly too. I will write again as soon as I can. We all send our love to you and Papa.

Sincerely,
William Jansen

I sat down on the floor weeping for the loss of my father. Mr. Macky sat down beside me and placed his arm around my shoulder to comfort me. I told him that I knew the loving and compassionate soul of my father would live on in my heart and the hearts of everyone he had touched. Losing him was the hardest loss I ever had to endure. Mr. Macky was such a nice Christian man, he prayed with me right there in the middle of the post office floor. When I returned home I read the letter to James. He also cried for my father. He loved him almost as much as I did. We gathered the family together to tell them of the sad news. We spent that evening praying for him, my mother, William, and the rest of the family. Although we had no other details of their trip, we knew it must have been a terrible experience.

We did get some scattered information from other people whose families made the fateful trip. Their letters were a little more informative than William's. They said thousands died on the trail. The pain endured on that trail would never be fully understood by anyone, except those who were there. The trail became known as the "Trail Of Tears."

The tribe did establish a new home for themselves in Indian Territory, which became known as the state of Oklahoma. They immediately began creating the New Cherokee Nation. They continued to be harassed by the United States government and others who tried to take their new land. They were more determined and fought even harder than before. The lives lost to get there would not be lost in vain, they would see to that. The resilience of the Cherokee was a testament to their character and ability to move onward in spite of prejudice and deprivation.

We received letters periodically from William, but he never talked about what they endured on what the Cherokee called the Nunna daul Tsuny, "The Trail Where They Cried." He spoke only of the work they had been doing to build homes and keep the white laws from invading their Sovereign Nation again.

After a couple of years, William sent a letter to tell us they were coming back to see us. I was so surprised. I never dreamed they would be able to return even for a visit. William didn't believe there was any danger as long as they kept to themselves and didn't wander into town.

James and I began getting ready for their return. We cleaned every wall and baseboard in the house. We had the grandchildren working to help us get everything perfect. My heart was so filled with joy. I was going to see my family again.

On the day the wagons pulled in, we were standing there waiting on the front porch. I ran to meet them before the horses had completely stopped. I helped my mother from the wagon and wrapped my arms around her tightly. I didn't want to let her go. She looked so worn and broken. Her skin was wrinkled and her eyes looked tired and weary. She barely smiled at me. William said she had been that way since my father died. I helped her inside and made her comfortable in the old rocking chair my father made for us when we moved into the house. I then went to hold my son. I held his face in my hands and just admired him. He was as handsome as the first day he came into this world. Those eyes were still the same vibrant blue. As always I was so proud to call him my son.

The girls and I prepared a huge supper for us all. I made some chestnut flatbread especially for my mother, as it was her favorite. When she saw it and tasted it, she looked up at me. There it was, that beautiful smile she had before she left here.

We had set up tents in the yard so everyone had a place to sleep. Besides my mother and William, my brothers, sisters, their wives and husbands, plus all my nieces and nephews had come. I was overjoyed to have them all back here for a little while.

We spent a wonderful two weeks together. The sparkle came back into my mother's eyes. She was at peace in this place that was once her homeland. We were not bothered by anyone. It was as though God had a wall of protection built around our property so no one could see inside. It was our little piece of paradise.

When the time came for them to leave again, the mood was very somber. James and I very slowly helped them load the wagons. We didn't want them to go. It was more difficult for them than it was for us. William said, "As agonizing as it is for us to leave, it is better for us in Oklahoma than it is here. We are no longer accepted in Georgia, and we wouldn't be safe. Out west is where the tribe lives, and that is our home." Just as he said those words, I felt that old familiar pang of guilt rising up from my belly.

I helped my mother into the wagon. She kissed me gently and rubbed my cheek as she said good-bye. I felt in my soul that would be our last good-bye, and it was. She died shortly after they returned to Oklahoma. I had to accept yet another heartache. It was her wisdom and courage that had been passed down to me. It was the lessons she taught that helped me to endure all that had been placed before me. She was a true Cherokee woman and mother.

William and the family came back to visit as often as they could. James and I went out there a few times. It was not an easy journey. Each time I tried to imagine what it was like for them on the trail during that horrible winter when Father lost his life and Mother lost her husband. I think she really died that day, too.

~ The Enchanted Land ~

The New Cherokee Nation was an extraordinary place to see. To view all that had been done by the tribe to start their lives over was miraculous. We were able to watch William give speeches before the Council. He had such a commanding presence. He was the epitome of leadership within the nation.

The Ever Growing Jansen Family

*Amongst years of turmoil and heartbreak
the cycle of life moves forever forward.*

By 1840, all our children were married except for William. When each child married, James and I gave them ten acres of land. Our family was close together, tribal like, just the way we wanted it.

John married at twenty. He married a very well-bred woman from a wealthy family. Her name was Jerusha, and she was from Buncombe, North Carolina. John met her on a trip there to deliver some lumber. They gave us four grandchildren, two girls and two boys.

James, Jr. was married at twenty-three to an older woman of twenty-six. Her name was Elizabeth. She had previously been married at nineteen but was widowed at twenty-four. Her first husband was thrown from a horse and died from his injuries a short time later. That union created a little boy whom we all loved, and James, Jr. became his Papa. They had three more children, all boys.

Jacob and Elijah both married local girls. We had known their families for years. Jacob and his wife Sally had four children, three girls and a boy.

Elijah's wife was Clara Mae. They had five children, two girls and three boys. Our family kept getting larger and larger.

Thomas had met a girl from across town named Irene. She was such a treasure, and he knew it. She was quiet and timid with such a sweet, tender nature. We all adored her, but we didn't understand why she never spoke of her family. She and Thomas never went to her home. They always came to ours. We were curious, but we didn't push the issue.

Every Sunday we would attend the Bells Baptist Church. The entire family would go, including Irene. It took four wagons when the Jansens went to church. No one around had a family the size of ours, especially a family that all went to church together. James' nephew, Abe, was the preacher. Everyone there loved our family, but we overheard them talking sometimes, saying that they wished we all wouldn't come at the same time because we took up so many pews. Our brood took up over half the church. We were hurt by their whispers, but it didn't stop us from piling in there every week.

After the sermon one Sunday, Abe announced that we were going to have a church building project. His exact words were, "We are going to build an extension to the sanctuary, and all the Jansens are going to help. The women will be providing food, so everyone is asked to be here at eight o'clock next Saturday morning."

We all looked at each other and then looked at him. James stood up and said, "My family would be honored to build the extension to the church, and my wife would be honored to feed everyone who comes out to assist us."

Although it was unexpected, we were so pleased. That was the ideal answer to the problem, especially since our massive family was the problem. The number of people who showed up to help was immense. It was finished that day, and every person there left with full stomachs from all the food we had made. It was God's hands at work again.

One Sunday after church we were getting ready to eat dinner on the porch, and a man came riding up on horse-back. He began screaming at Irene to get on the horse. Thomas told us it was her father. He demanded Irene go home with him. Thomas politely told the gentleman, "Sir, Irene is staying for dinner. You are welcome to join us."

The man said, "I will not stay for dinner, and my daughter will no longer be cavorting with the likes of you. I can't believe you bunch of half-breeds have been able to stay here. I will not allow my daughter to keep company with your son."

I started to jump up and say my piece, but James stopped me. He stood up instead and said, "Mister, you will not talk about my family that way. I want you off my property."

Irene spoke up. "I won't go with you. I love Thomas and his family, and we will be getting married." Her father then told her she would no longer be his daughter or wel-comed in his home.

I could see how hurt she was by his words, but she told him straightforward, "Then I guess you are no longer my father."

He took off on his horse and Thomas yelled, "By the way, my mother is no half-breed. She is a full-blood Cherokee!"

Poor Irene was distraught for a few days, but she knew she was loved by us. We became her family. She and Thomas were married and had five children, three girls and two boys. It was a good thing we built onto the church.

Being a woman from two different worlds was harder than anyone could have imagined. Over the years I met other Cherokee women who had married white men. They also stayed behind while their families were forced to leave. We got together at least once a month to comfort and support each other. Of course, we had to do this very discreetly. We didn't want anyone in town to see a group of Indian women together. There was so much prejudice among a lot of the whites, and they would use any opportunity to harass those of us still in Georgia. We met at each other's homes and were never seen. Our meetings gave me a sense of being in the world of the Cherokee. It helped knowing I was not alone.

Lucinda was so much like William. While I was having my get-togethers with the other Cherokee women in our town, she was having her own secret rendezvous with the children of these women. They met once a month in a barn at the back of our property. She always cooked a huge meal to take down there for her friends. She also wanted to be a part of her Cherokee heritage in whatever way she could.

She fell in love with the son of one of my friends. Joseph was one-quarter Cherokee, and he was so handsome. He had many Cherokee characteristics—dark hair and eyes and that bronze skin.

They were married and had two children, twin boys. We had never known anyone who had twins. I was so shocked after one was born and the doctor said there was another one. Our Lucinda had such a hard time delivering those babies. There was no shaman around then, so all we had was the town doctor and, as always, prayers. She was a tough young woman, and after many hours of dreadful labor, she birthed two small but healthy children. It was like seeing her at birth all over again. Like their mother, those children were very special.

William Shares the Untold Story

Truth is the unveiling of necessary pain
Healing is hidden within the truth
It cannot be concealed forever

W illiam was still unmarried. We had become resolved to the fact that our oldest child would never give us a grandchild. He was heavily involved in the workings of the Cherokee Nation in Oklahoma, so he still had no time for courting. Although we wanted him to marry and have children, we were very proud of all he had done for my people. He made a lifelong commitment to stand for the Cherokee. He never gave up the fight for the

God-given rights of all Native Americans.

James and I were constantly surrounded by all our grandchildren, and we loved every moment of it. They kept us feeling young. We had so many, and each of them had a special place in our hearts. James and I could no longer play stick ball or chase after them like we used to, but we adored watching them play. One or two of them would periodically run over to me, already puckered for a kiss, shouting, "I love you, Grandma Lu." My heart would just quiver with delight. It gave me such pleasure when they would simultaneously yell, "Papa James, look at me." I would see his face glow with elation over whatever it was they had done. They gave the both of us so much joy in our old age.

Our love for each other grew more with each passing day. It seemed the older we got, the better we were together, if that was possible. Just holding hands and kissing could bring us the same intense feelings as passionate lovemaking had in our younger years. After the children and grandchildren would go back to their own homes, James and I would spend our quiet evenings on the front porch swing. We would sit arm in arm watching the beautiful night sky. I would rest my head gently on his shoulder as he rested his head gently on mine. The moments like those had always defined the depth of our love.

In 1844, William surprised us with an unannounced visit. We opened the door and there he was, standing next to a beautiful Indian woman with a baby in her arms. We knew without asking she was his wife and that was his child. James and I began shouting hallelujahs and dancing around like a couple of spring chickens. After we calmed ourselves down, he introduced us to his wife, Annie. He then told us the little girl's name. Luiza Bluebird Jansen. He had named her after me. I couldn't stop crying. I felt I was given the greatest honor a mother could ever receive from a son. William had finally given us a lovely daughter-in-law and a sweet, sweet granddaughter.

William had married a full-blood Indian woman. That meant the Cherokee blood would flow even stronger among the descendents of James and me. We had truly come full circle.

William said he had another reason for coming to see us. He was ready to tell the story of what happened to them during the removal. He asked that I gather the rest of the family. He wanted them all to hear it.

Once everyone was there, we sat on the front porch. It

was amazing to see my family and extended family all together. William sat in the rocking chair looking very solemn as he began to speak.

He said the day the soldiers came for them they were ready. They had prepared a trunk filled with blankets and other essentials they might need. They thought they would be able to take a wagon, so they had one hitched and ready to go. The soldiers had other plans. They forced them at gunpoint to leave their home. They were only allowed to take the trunk, which had to be carried. As they were climbing up the mountain just up from the house, they turned to see a devastating sight. The soldiers who remained behind were stealing the horses and burning down the house. My mother fainted at the sight of those horrific men destroying her home. William said my father had to carry her to the top of the mountain. The family was then led to a stockade in Tennessee, where they were held until the journey west.

The stockades were filled with other Indian families. The government provided them with rations, but it wasn't enough to feed everyone. Many gave up their rations to the children. Those who had blankets shared with those who didn't. Every night someone else would become ill and soon after would die. Disease spread like wildfire within the confines of the stockades. Death had no mercy. It came upon men, women, and children, the young and the old. They lived that way for months until the day they were herded into wagons. There weren't enough wagons or horses, and the men would walk so the women and children could ride.

The journey west had begun, but not without more devastation for our people. The weather was bitter cold, and the wind blew with such force it stung as it hit your skin. Every day several people would die from the elements.

William's voice changed as he told of my father's death. It was the most difficult for him to share. He told us that my father had walked for days since giving up his seat on the wagon to a frail and sickly man. He said my father had a terrible cough and wasn't breathing well, so a younger man gave up his seat for him. They placed him in the wagon under some warm blankets, but the pneumonia was more than he could fight. A medicine man was on the wagon in front of them. He came back and stayed with my father and prayed over him, but within four days he was dead.

Several of the men dug a shallow grave alongside the

Mississippi River. William wasn't sure where they were, and he said he had been unable to find the grave since. He assured me that they said Christian prayers when they buried him and asked God to give him a place next to all the other great men who had passed before him.

He went on to say the tribe was in danger from more than illness. Just passing through the towns placed the Indians at risk. Many white families would stand along the trail and spit at them, calling them unthinkable names. Some of the Cherokee men retaliated and were killed. They could no longer take the humiliation that had been heaped upon them. Death was a better alternative.

William then asked his father and me to forgive him for what he was about to tell us. He said that one night, while everyone slept, a white man came into camp and grabbed a young girl, placing his hand over her mouth so she couldn't scream. He dragged her to the woods. William said he quietly followed them. The man had already begun hurting the child when William attacked him from behind, pulling the man away from the little girl. He slit the man's throat from ear to ear and hid the body under some brush. He told the girl never to tell anyone. She promised and thanked him for saving her. He took her safely back to her family, who were still sleeping. He said he prayed all night for God to forgive him for taking another life. He had not told anyone this story and swore us to secrecy. We all knew that William could have been killed for murdering a white man. James and I personally knew what it meant to keep secrets. We told William there was nothing for us to forgive. He did the right thing by protecting that child.

I asked William to tell me why my sister Mary had such a terrible limp. She never would say what happened to her leg. He said she had not spoken of the journey since they arrived in Indian Territory all those years ago. He said she had fallen from the wagon and broken her leg. They tied a stick around it to hold it in place. She cried and screamed for days. Fortunately, no infection set in, but by the time they got there, the bone had fused incorrectly. Her leg was left terribly deformed. My heart went out to her. She carried the trauma of that journey deep inside her, and I know the pain that can cause.

William said a prayer of blessings and thanksgiving. In his prayer he thanked God that I was his mother. When he opened his eyes, he looked into mine and shared one last thing. He said my father's dying last words were to tell me he was proud that I was his daughter, and he would understand if I were ever forced to break my promise in order to survive. He said I should never be ashamed of myself.

I didn't tell William that I had been placed in such a position, that I had in fact deceived my father in more ways than one. I just couldn't share that with him.

My wise son said to me, "Mother, living in two worlds as you have done for so long has had difficulties of its own that no one could understand unless they also lived there. You have undergone so much pain and heartache, yet you never let it stop you from your God-given duty to care for us and teach us in the ways we should go. You did this with grace in spite of what was going on inside you. I have always viewed you as a Cherokee woman of strength and courage, with enough love for not just one world, but two. I am honored to be your son."

I cherished his words, but I still felt my sins were unpardonable. William and his wife and child returned to Oklahoma. He became the great man we always knew he would be. He never stopped, he was on every board, attended every meeting. Annie said he was hardly ever home. She said he was a warrior, a mighty advocate for the Cherokee people and highly revered by the entire Cherokee Nation.

Oh, My Grieving Soul

This loss is more than I can bear
Can I survive again?
Will you heal my grieving soul?
I must trust in you

We received a letter from Oklahoma. James and I couldn't open it fast enough. We always became so excited when we received a letter from William. This time the letter wasn't from William, but from Annie.

Dear James and Lu,

I am writing you with a grieving heart. You both know how hard William has worked in his life and always with the determination of a raging bull. I guess his heart just couldn't keep up with the pace. It just stopped beating in the middle of the night. He didn't suffer. He went peacefully to be with the Lord. By the time you receive this letter we will have buried him. Please know I will follow his wishes for his funeral. He will be buried here in the burial ground with many other Cherokees who have served this community, this Nation.

I want to thank you for raising the most wonderful man and loving father I have ever known. I will always be grateful and so will Luiza. She loved her father so much. We are getting through this heartbreaking time as best we can. Please don't worry about us. We will come to visit as soon as possible.

I pray God will give you peace during your time of grief. William loved you both very much.

Please take comfort in knowing that he had such a profound effect on many lives here in the Cherokee Nation. As I am writing this letter to you they have already begun building a memorial in his honor.

You raised an amazing and inspiring son. The Cherokee Nation sends their condolences and their thanks as well.

With Love,
Annie and Luiza

I couldn't breathe. I felt as if my own heart had stopped beating. James began shaking me as the tears poured from his eyes. When the breath came from me, it came as a guttural moan and then a scream of sheer agony. I collapsed to the floor. There was only enough energy left within me to cry more tears than I ever thought possible. I didn't have the strength to stand. James and I sat there holding each other as we sobbed. Losing my father wouldn't be my most difficult loss after all. It would be losing my son. We never thought one of our children would go before we did.

In the weeks that followed, we mourned for our precious William, but we had the privilege of seeing him become exactly the man he was destined to be. He showed by example that through endurance, stamina, and faith, any adversity could be overcome. Although our beloved son was dead, he left behind a legacy that would live on in all future generations of Cherokees.

A few months later, Annie and Luiza came to visit. It was as though God had given us William back through his daughter. She was just like her father, high-spirited and anxious about everything. If something needed to be done, she was right on it. She knew what she wanted, and nothing could ever stand in her way. Annie said she had as hard a time keeping up with her as she had William. It is so remarkable how life goes on.

We went to Oklahoma to visit them once after William

died. Luiza was already following her father's path. She was teaching younger children the history of the Cherokees and the wondrous land from which they came. She told the story of their journey to Oklahoma. James and I believed that she could grow up to become the Principal Chief of the Cherokee Nation.

The Journey's End

I have taken a long and incredible journey but
I have not been alone; the Lord was with me.
When the weight of my sins caused me to fall,
He picked me up and presented me with forgive-
ness. When I couldn't go forward he pushed me;
many times he carried me. He created me just as I
am, and no one can take that away.

J ames and I had seen many changes in the lives of the
Cherokee and in the lives of our family. We watched
our children develop into exceptional adults. We survived
the death of one of them with our faith still intact. We saw
our grandchildren grow up and were able to meet some of
our great-grandchildren. We had a full and rewarding life
together. We were abundantly blessed.

God also helped me to finally forgive myself. I came to realize I never meant to betray my parents or my people by the actions I took and the words I spoke as the Cherokee wife of a white man. It was a world ruled by hatred and greed that forced me to protect myself and my children.

In 1870, James suffered a stroke, which left him paralyzed and unable to speak or show emotion of any kind. It was the loneliest time of my life. I cared for him for eight long months. He had to be fed and bathed; he just lay there expressionless. I would speak to him constantly as though he were going to sit up and talk back to me, but he didn't. I began to pray for God to please bring my husband back to me or just take him on to his heavenly home. I couldn't bear to see him that way any longer.

One night as I sat by his bed, I saw something in his gorgeous blue eyes that I hadn't seen in a very long time. I went over to him and gently laid my head on his shoulder, as I had done so many times. To my surprise, he laid his head gently on mine and he spoke. "I love you, my little Indian princess, until we meet again." He kissed my forehead as he had always done. Then my beloved James was gone. Hearing his voice one last time was the most endearing gift God could have ever given me.

The love we shared in our long life together was un-paralleled—nothing could compare. That wonderful white man and I, an Indian woman, were an extension of each other. Ours was one of a kind, a portrait of love painted by the Creator God himself.

A few years after James passed, I became very ill. I had terrible pain in my stomach after I ate. Nothing I did made me feel any better. I tried sumac and yellow root. They helped to ease the pain temporarily. My herbal remedies had always worked in the past, but they didn't seem to work for me anymore. When I stopped eating al-together, I decided I should see the doctor. He listened to my stomach and pressed on it with his hands. He looked concerned. He then turned to me and said there was a very large growth inside of me. He told me there was nothing he could do and that it was growing so fast, death would probably come soon. I went home and told my children and grandchildren. They were all very distressed. I en-couraged them not to be sad, but to give thanks for the years we'd had together. I assured them I was ready to go and I was not afraid. Lucinda hugged me and said she wanted to take care of me until I passed. I told her that would please me very much.

Lucinda has been by my side through the entire ordeal. She is a great help to me. I have never drunk liquor in my life, but now it is my only form of pain relief. That sweet daughter of mine makes sure I have a bottle by my bed at all times. I could not have prepared for my coming departure without her. We pray together several times a day so that I may have the strength to complete this story. I have been telling her the words, and she has been writing them down for me.

I convinced Lucinda to go see her family so I could be alone for a while with my pen and paper. My strength is fading, but I will try to finish.

As I lie here looking out my window at the beautiful Georgia sky, I realize the grace that has been bestowed upon me. I have always loved the land where I was born, and I've been privileged to be able to call it home. I have full understanding of the purpose God had for my staying here. This land is no longer the Enchanted Land of my ancestors, but because of my marriage to James and the children we bore, there will be Cherokees walking on this Georgia soil for generations to come.

It is now my time to go to another home that has been

prepared for me. I thank you for allowing me to share my story. As I take my last breath of life, I leave you with these, my final words. "I am Luiza Bluebird Jansen. I am Cherokee."

An Afterword from the Author

I hope you enjoyed reading my book. It was my imagination working to create a story that could have been true for my family and many others. I know without a doubt there were many Native American women who stayed in Georgia while their families were forced to leave. I believe those who stayed behind endured their own hardships.

If stories have been passed down in your family about an infamous Cherokee grandmother, they are probably true. If you decide to research it, you will not regret it. I have so much respect for my ancestors now. I am honored to be a Native American descendant.

I wrote this book in honor of all the Native American women who stayed behind and then passed down the story to each generation, so that she was still known years later as someone's Cherokee grandmother, someone's Luiza Bluebird.

Acknowledgements

There are many to whom I would like to offer thanks. For their privacy I will only use their first names. They know who they are. My heartfelt thanks go out to:

Andy, Tammy, Donna, the Debbies, Belinda, and all the wonderful people at Point of Need Ministries. You showed me what it felt like to be accepted, just as I am. Thanks for encouraging me to go forward with this book.

Tammy, my Cherokee friend, for inspiring me to begin my Native American research.

All the people at my job who put up with me after long sleepless nights and my constant ramblings about this book. Many thanks to Leslie for pushing me to do more, and proofreading my manuscript. Your suggestions and encouragement were indispensable.

Karen M. for leading me in a direction that introduced me to courage I didn't know I had.

Debbie G., Sherri G., Bart G., and Tina A., for always loving and believing in me.

To all my other friends who have indirectly helped to support me in ways that led me where I am today. (You all know who you are and that I love you.)

Mom and Robin, for your support and for just plain loving me. I love you both so much.

Kelly, my brother, just because I love you.

My children and grandchildren, Brittany, Corey, Jaxson, and Knox: you give me the most joy in my life. I love you all!!

All my family members who have supported my writing and my research over the years. Myra, Diane, Dana, Bobby, Aunt Cat, Tommy (who has passed away), Debbie, Cheryl, and a slew of others. You also know who you are. Without your help, this wouldn't have been possible.

If I have left anyone out, please accept my apologies and know I love you all.

Without your encouragement, love, and faith in my ability, I could not have written this book. I am so grateful to each one of you.

Most importantly, I would like to thank God for loving me so much that he gave me a gift and a purpose in this journey called life. I thank him for always giving me his unconditional love. I look forward to the rest of our journey together.

The Bluebird Spirit

I am the Bluebird.

My spirit still flies over these Native Lands.

I touch the treetops with my wings,

I hear the rolling waters of the rivers and streams.

It's as though nothing has changed,

but everything has changed.

I can hear the voices of those who suffered

on the long journey to the new land.

I hear their cries as they look to the sky,

What will be ahead of us?

A barren desert, with no flowers, or shades of green.

Will we have peace in that place?

Oh, wind and rain,

Oh, Great Creator God, hear our pleas!

Carry us to the place we belong.

Come take our hand and lead us backward in time,

back to our Enchanted Land.

Printed in the United States
126739LV00001B/5/P